ALEX SHAW

HETMAN DONETSK CALLING

ALEX SHAW

Published in the USA with consent from Hetman Publishing

Date of first UK publication August 2012

Copyright © Alexander William Shaw 2012

The right of 'Alex Shaw' to be identified as the author
of this work has been asserted by him in accordance with the
Copyright Designs and Patents Act 1988.

This is a work of fiction.
All names, characters, places and incidents, other than those which are public domain, are the product of the author's imagination or are used fictitiously and any resemblance to actual persons, living or dead, businesses, events, or locales is entirely coincidental.

All rights reserved.
This book is sold subject to the condition that it shall not, by way of trade or otherwise, be reproduced, stored in a retrieval system, be lent, resold, hired out, or otherwise circulated or transmitted without the author's prior consent in any form of binding or cover other than that in which it is published and without a similar condition, including this condition, being imposed on the subsequent purchaser.

First published in the United Kingdom by Hetman Publishing
www.hetmanpublishing.com
Date of first US publication August 2012
ISBN-13 978-0956159250

HETMAN: DONETSK CALLING

This book is dedicated to my wife Galia,
my sons Alexander & Jonathan
and my family in England and Ukraine.

ALEX SHAW

ALEX SHAW was head of Drama at Pechersk School International, Kyiv, Ukraine, in the late 1990's before leaving to start his own Kyiv based 'consultancy' dealing specifically with the markets of the former USSR. He was subsequently head hunted for a division of Siemens where he was tasked with business development in the former USSR, the Middle East and Africa. Hetman was Alex's first novel and took twelve years to complete. Published in 2009 it gained critical acclaim in the 2010 Amazon Breakthrough Novel Award (ABNA) and later became a #1 UK Kindle bestseller. Cold Black was published a year later. It followed the success of Hetman, gaining critical acclaim in ABNA 2011 and rose to #6 in the Kindle UK bestseller list. Both books have also now become top 10 Kindle Bestsellers in the USA. In July 2012 Cold Black became a #1 German Kindle bestseller; Hetman reached #4 in April. The third Aidan Snow thriller will be released in November 2012.

When not writing Alex works as a freelance consultant (clients include the UN), dividing his time between his two homes in Kyiv, Ukraine and West Sussex, England. He is married to his beautiful wife Galia and has two fantastic sons, Alexander and Jonathan.

Alex welcomes feedback and comments from readers and can be contacted via his website www.alexwshaw.com you can also follow Alex on twitter: @alexshawhetman

HETMAN: DONETSK CALLING

Praise for Alex Shaw

'He won't be stopped now. The book will become popular among Kyiv's expats; some of them will even recognize themselves.' **Kyiv Post on 'Hetman'**

'A strong aspect of **HETMAN** is Shaw's knowledge of Ukraine & Special Forces operations. The character of Bull felt real on the page, you don't get better than that.'
2010 Amazon Breakthrough Novel Award Review

'Thrillers really aren't my cup of tea…but I loved this!!!'
2011 Amazon Breakthrough Novel Award Review

ALEX SHAW

HETMAN DONETSK CALLING

This short story was written entirely on location in Ukraine and the UK in August 2012.

HETMAN: DONETSK CALLING

Kyiv, Ukraine

Brian Webb swayed as he hailed a taxi. It was the early hours of the morning and he'd been drinking since the early evening. The heat of the day had long since given way to the chill of the night. Webb shivered in his short sleeved shirt and cargo shorts. Within seconds a battered, yellow Daewoo Nubira pulled into the curb. The driver lowered the front passenger window and then with a price agreed Webb climbed into the back. It was four a.m. as they sped along the all but deserted city streets. Even by his standards this had been a late night, Webb chuckled to himself. Life was good. He had a great life in Kyiv, a great wife and a great daughter. What more could he want? He let his eye lids drop as the taxi moved from tarmac to cobbles and headed downhill towards the Dnipro River. The vibration made his stomach wobble and his head nod. Webb had arrived in Ukraine in October 1997 with only four words of Russian 'Da', 'Niet', 'Babushka' and 'Vodka' but had somehow managed not only to survive but thrive. Not passing for a local, with his thick

Yorkshire accent but being accepted as one by his neighbours, he would be sad to leave his adopted home. He opened his eyes as the taxi crossed the river and wound down the window slightly, breathing in the river cooled air. His eyes met those of the driver who quickly looked away. The man seemed to be in no mood to talk. The taxi continued on across the bridge, through Hydropark and then onto Levo Berezna – Kyiv's left bank.

The taxi abruptly pulled in at the side of the road. Webb sat forward and looked around. It wasn't his street. The driver quickly got out and walked away. His brain slowed by alcohol, Webb remained seated for several seconds before he realised that something was wrong. He hauled his bulk out of the car and leant against the door. As Webb stared at the driver, the Ukrainian looked back and then broke into a run. Webb heard footsteps behind and turned around. It was then that he saw them, illuminated in the eerie glow of the street lights. About twenty feet away a group of four large men were heading directly for him. Webb watched mesmerised for a moment before his eyes focussed on the baseball bats two of them were carrying. The nearest figure pointed at him and then the group broke into a run. Webb felt his pulse quicken. He was defenceless. He looked down and saw that the keys to the taxi were still in the ignition. Without giving it a second thought he clambered into the driver's seat, took the hand-break off and spun the taxi away from the curb. He heard shouts and then a loud crack as something hit the rear of the taxi. Webb's heart started to beat raggedly; it felt as though it was trying to escape from his chest. He forced the Daewoo to accelerate away and squinted to focus on the road ahead. He was now sweating; his hands wet on the wheel. He chanced a look back and saw that there were lights behind him, following him. What was happening, why was he being chased? Webb had no idea. He shot through a set of traffic lights narrowly missing a large tanker. He knew the roads now, he wasn't too far from home but he couldn't lead them there. The road swung in and out of focus as the alcohol refused to leave his system, Webb was heavy on the controls and the car jerked as he changed down to negotiate a bend. He clipped a parked car with his wing mirror, the glass shattered as it was ripped off. The chase lights he now saw belonged to a large BMW and were getting closer. His breathing became heavier. Thoughts raced through his mind; who were they...what did they want...

He reached the highway that dissected the Harkivskiy Massif district and saw lit up by the neon lights of the Billa Supermarket signage a Lada Samara with Militia markings. Webb aimed for it. As he slowed and drew near he saw that it was empty. Webb banged his fist on the wheel in frustration and was about to curse when there was a loud crack and something pinged off of the Daewoo. He ducked, he had never heard gunfire before but instantly realised that was what the noise had been. Whoever was chasing him had started to shoot! He floored the accelerator. The Daewoo jerked forward cresting the curb and across the car-park, before bouncing over the grass verge and back onto the tarmac. A grating noise started to come from the front suspension as Webb thrashed the car back up the gears. He saw a gap in the central reservation, snapped the steering wheel to the left and crossed to the other side of the road, changing direction. He urged the taxi to go faster, he had to get away. The Daewoo started to vibrate angrily as it reached the 100k mark. He wiped the sweat from his brow. There were a few more cars about now as he continued along the main road back towards the river. He looked in the rear-view mirror and couldn't see anyone following him. He let out a deep breath and relaxed slightly as the adrenalin started to leave his system. It was now almost five a.m. and a wave of tiredness rolled over him. His eyes closed...the Daewoo violently shook and bucked. Webb's eyes snapped open. He had driven off the road. Too late to avoid the bus stop, Webb folded his arms in front of his face. His head hit hard and he blacked out.

Webb tried to understand where he was as the world swum back into focus. He slithered out of the crumpled car. His eyes stung. He wiped them with his hands and saw blood now covering his palms. Pulling a handkerchief out of his pocket he dabbed at his eyes again. Webb looked back and saw that the passenger side of the car had been concertinaed, taking the brunt of the impact. He was lucky to be alive. It was a Saturday morning and the pavement was still empty as he tried to walk. His left ankle gave way and he all but fell. He hobbled from the scene of the accident still not knowing what to do. On the other side of the road he saw a large dark blue BMW saloon stop. Two men got out and started to run across the road dodging the light traffic whilst the car moved off again looking for somewhere to cross. Webb took a deep breath, put his head down and tried to run. He was fifty-six, overweight and drunk…and the pain in his foot was excruciating but he managed to move. He loped away from the road and towards the nearest block of flats. Reaching the monolithic high rise he clambered up the five steps to the entrance hall and went straight out of the other side. He was in a courtyard created by four apartment blocks facing each other. In the middle there was a small children's play area. He bumped past the slide and into the entrance hall of the next block. The building was very much like his. He called the lift, was surprised to see it worked and sent it to the top floor as he ducked around the side of the lift shaft and hid in the shadows by the entrance to the maintenance room. He hunched over, panting. All was quiet apart from the sound of his chest heaving. He vomited as waves of pain roared through his body. He couldn't go home; he couldn't go to the Militia. He had no other choice; there was only one person who could help, one man he knew would not let him down. He pulled out his old Nokia and called Aidan Snow.

HETMAN: DONETSK CALLING

Worthing, United Kingdom.

Aidan Snow slowed his pace as he felt his Blackberry vibrate in his zip pocket. He retrieved the device and saw that it was an incoming call from one of his closest friends, a friend however he had not seen for too long. Snow answered the call and started to walk.
"Brian Webb, how are you?"
"Aidan is that you?"
"Er yes. Don't tell me you're pissed already? What time is it in Kyiv, eight a.m.?"
Webb' voice was rushed and his breathing laboured. "Aidan I need your help I don't know what to do – they are threatening me and the family."
Snow stopped and placed his right foot on a bench to stretch his ham strings. "Brian take a breath and tell me what's happening?"
"Aidan I've got to keep moving they've found me..." Webb stopped talking abruptly and Snow could hear raised voices at the other end and banging.
"Brian. Brian are you still there?"
"Aidan can you come to Kyiv? Can you get here quickly? I need you to help..."
"Brian...Brian!"
As Snow looked out to sea he could hear Brian speaking to someone then he heard a yell and what sounded like a crashing sound. Suddenly a deep voice came on the phone and asked in Russian. "Who is this?"
Snow replied in English. "Is Brian there?"
The voice switched to heavily accented English. "Yes." The line went dead.
Snow redialled and the call went to voicemail, Brian's voicemail. "Brian call me when you can." Snow looked up Brian's home number, hoped it hadn't changed and dialled. He let it ring for a minute before disconnecting. Snow frowned, he

could count his number of true friends on one hand and Brian was one of them. Brian now owned a chain of English language book shops in Kyiv, but it had been before this that Snow had met him. They had both been teaching at the same international school and Snow was the 'new boy'. Brian had taken Snow under his wing. The Yorkshire man was twenty years Snow's senior but the age gap had not made a jot of difference especially to Brian's pretty wife Katya who was younger than Snow. He had never heard the happy Yorkshire man speak like that before. Still carrying the guilt of failing to save one friend years before Snow had vowed never to let it happen again. Snow dialled his boss' number.

"Patchem." A voice said after four rings.

"It's Aidan, sorry for calling you this early on a Saturday."

Jack Patchem, Snow's controller at the Secret Intelligence Service (SIS) too sounded out of breath. "Not at all. Ok, I'm listening."

"Jack I need to take a few days off, some of that holiday time I'm owed."

"You are asking for a Holiday?"

"No something's come up, a personal matter."

On the golf course Patchem raised his eyebrows. "Anything that I should know about?"

"No. I just need to help a friend out."

"So from the timing of this call I expect you need it immediately? Yes?"

"Yes."

"Go, but make sure you can get back if I need you."

"Thanks." Snow ended the call and then tried both of Brian's numbers again; neither was answered by a human. Snow put his Blackberry back into his zip and pocket and ran the remaining mile home along the promenade. Back indoors he quickly purchased a ticket online for the next flight to Kyiv, which on this occasion happened to be with Ukraine International Airlines before taking a quick shower. Dressed in khaki combats, dark blue polo shirt and a pair of UK Gear PT1000s; he collected his 'grab-bag' before leaving the house and rapidly driving to Gatwick.

Gatwick Airport, United Kingdom

Ukraine International Airlines flight 502 would not get Snow to Kyiv until late afternoon but was the earliest available. Snow had been forced to pay a premium for a business class seat but money was not on his mind. What was bothering him was Brian Webb and what may or may not have happened to him. He again had tried both of Brian's phone numbers but to no avail. He'd spent the three hours he'd had to wait until his flight boarded snoozing in the business lounge and reading the latest Stephen Leather 'Spider Shepherd' Thriller. Now as they took off he found himself sitting next to a businessman in a tight fitting suit. After the pre-flight drinks were served Snow's neighbour, who'd ordered a double Scotch, introduced himself.
"Cheers! Donald Bass, Don to my friends."
Snow tried not to let his amusement at the man's name show.
"Aidan Snow."
"Nice to meet you. I know it's a cliché but business or pleasure?"
"Personal."
"Not internet dating? I've heard the women there are quite tasty!"
"They are but I'm just going to help a friend. I used to live there."
"I've never been. I'm meeting my Ukrainian business partner he owns a few bars but now wants to open a 'fish and chip' shop." Bass handed Snow a business card. "Yep that's me 'Bass' Plaice'. I'm now selling the franchise internationally."
"I think it will do well."
"Do you mind if I pick your brain?"

"No." Snow was glad of the distraction.

"Is it Kiev or Kyiv? Look this newspaper is 'The Kyiv Post' but my guidebook says 'Kiev'."

Snow remembered when 'The Kyiv Post' was 'The Kiev Post' but did not want to confuse issues. "Kiev is a translation from Russian but 'Kyiv' is from the Ukrainian."

"Oh. So what should I try to speak?"

"You can use either in Kyiv but Ukrainian is the official language."

Bass pointed at the paper. "But this report says that they have passed a law granting Russian second language status."

"In the East the majority of the population is of Russian descent so they prefer to speak Russian. And because the President is from the East he wants Russian to be used more. It's his first language."

"So it's a bit like Wales then? In Cardiff they speak English but go north and it's all Yaki-da?"

"Yes."

"I get you. It mentions here 'Bandits from Donetsk'. Are there a lot of mafia types in Kyiv? Should I be worried?"

"I lived there for a few years and never saw any trouble." Snow lied but then his experience of Ukraine had not been unusual. "In the early nineties they had problems of course but that all got worked out. Kyiv is very safe, the new President has brought his cronies in from the East but as a foreign businessman they'll welcome you. At the end of the day people are people, regardless of where they are from or what language they speak."

"I see. So what are the women like?"

"Most of them have two legs."

Bass started to laugh noisily as the cabin crew started their safety demonstration and then readied themselves for take-off. As soon as the plane levelled out Bass ordered another double scotch and then fell asleep. Snow tried to doze again but his mind was too troubled.

HETMAN: DONETSK CALLING

Levo Berezna, Kyiv, Ukraine

Snow paid the taxi driver and climbed into the entrance to Brian Webb's apartment block. As usual the Soviet era building was grimy and smelt vaguely of rubbish. Snow pressed the lift button and hoped that it worked. Brian had once joked that he lived in a penthouse. His flat may well have been on the eighteenth floor but it was certainly no penthouse. With a jolt the lift doors opened and Snow was jerkily taken to the top floor. As the doors closed Snow turned left and found the correct flat. He pressed the bell, which sounded like a strange kind of Chinese bird and waited. The door remained closed. He listened, heard nothing, and then rang again. There were noises from inside and then it was suddenly pulled open. Snow could not help but smile at the vision of Katya dripping wet clad in nothing but a bath towel. He still had no clue how Brian had pulled her.
"Aidan!" Her frown turned to a smile and she stepped forward and hugged him.
"Katya." He dropped his holdall. He could feel her curves through the thin towel and had to remind himself that although she was gorgeous she was his friend's wife.
She moved away and looked up at him. "You look good. Come in."
"Thanks, so do you."
She smiled mischievously and as she turned he caught a flash of her bum as the towel rose up. Snow closed the door and followed her into the lounge. She sat and lit a cigarette.
"Is Brian here?" Snow thought he already knew the answer but had to ask.
Katya exhaled angrily. "No, he's bloody not."
In any other circumstance Snow would have laughed at Katya's use of language, clearly influenced by her husband. "Do you know where he is?"

She shrugged. "He was meant to pick us up from the central railway station this morning. We had to drag our bags to the taxi rank." She noticed Snow was frowning. "We went to Yalta for a week; Vika and I. You remember Vika?"

Snow nodded, she had big breasts and Brian had a nickname for her which he couldn't repeat. "So he wasn't with you and he didn't turn up at the station?"

"Yes. Aidan what's wrong, what are you doing here? I haven't seen you since after…"

"Arnaud was killed? It's OK, it's been four years. Look, Brian called me this morning and said he was in trouble, I've never heard him speak like that."

Katya now seemed more concerned that angry. "He's not come home some nights when he's been out drinking. Euro 2012 was awful, he met up with a group of England fans and Michael Jones; well you know Michael. I just thought that he'd done the same. I thought you were him at the door. Do you think something has happened to him?"

"That's what I'm trying to find out."

"You are a good friend Aidan for coming here."

They were both startled by the doorbell. Katya looked at Snow. He nodded and made for the door. He looked through the peep-hole and saw two men in uniform. He sensed something was not quite right; he put the chain on and opened the door.

"Hello can I help you?"

The two officers reminded Snow of Laurel and Hardy and looked a little confused by being faced by a foreigner. The nearest and much thinner of the two spoke. "Is Webb, Katya at home?" He asked in Russian before adding in English, "Please."

Snow continued to play the dumb foreign visitor. He did not want to let on that he spoke Russian fluently. "You want Katya, 'da'?"

"Da."

"Ok." Snow called back into the flat. "Katya the police are here and want to speak to you. I don't understand as I don't speak

Ukrainian." He was telling the truth, Russian was different enough.

Katya looked at Snow; eyebrows raised but made no comment. She had pulled on a long t-shirt dress. "Tak?" 'Yes' - she asked in Ukrainian.

Stan Laurel persisted with Russian and said. "Can we come in?"

"What is this about?" Katya too now used Russian.

"Your husband." Oliver Hardy stated.

"Come in."

Snow stepped aside as the two uniformed men entered the flat. They all went into the lounge. Katya took up her previous seat and lit a new cigarette.

"Who is this?" Oliver Hardy the older, more senior officer asked as he tilted his head towards Snow.

"A family friend. Now what is this about?"

"Your husband has been taken to our station for questioning." It was Stan Laurel, the younger officer again.

"About what?"

The older officer took over and Snow wondered if this was an attempt at 'Good Cop – Bad Cop'. "He has been identified as being at the scene of a very serious incident. We need you to tell us where he was yesterday."

"What kind of incident?"

"I am afraid that until we have investigated further I cannot tell you anymore."

"What kind of answer is that?" Katya's face flashed with anger. "I demand you tell me why you are holding him!"

"It really would be in your own best interests to answer the question." The younger officer smiled, as did Snow.

"Where was he yesterday?"

"He was here."

"With you?"

"No."

Oliver Hardy looked confused. "Where were you?"

"Yalta."

"So how do you know he was here?"

"I called him."

He nodded and pointed to the house phone. "On that number?"

"Yes, I mean no. I called his mobile."

"And he said he was here?"

"Yes." She could feel herself starting to redden.

"So how do you know he was really here?"

Snow cut in, still using English. "Anyone for tea, or coffee or perhaps 'sto gram'?"

"Ask him to be quiet please." The older officer asked Katya.

"Do it yourself."

He didn't. Stan Laurel pointed at Snow. "Mister, quiet please."

Snow smiled, the officer now sounded more like a young, homosexual Borat. "Oh, sorry."

"So how do you know he was here or not?"

Katya did not reply straight away but let the smoke flow out of her mouth. "Have you informed the British Embassy that you have arrested my husband?"

"He has not been arrested."

"So he is free to leave?"

"No."

"I don't understand."

The older officer abruptly stood. "It is difficult. He is being questioned."

Katya stood and stabbed her finger in the man's direction. "I demand you let him go."

The officer's face changed and Snow sensed that violence may be on his mind. "You are in no position to make any demands! In fact I may have to arrest you for obstructing a police investigation."

"Please just answer our questions." The younger officer pleaded.

Snow stood and readied himself for a physical confrontation. "So how many was that for tea? Milk and sugar?"

"Shut up!" The older officer spat in Russian. "Now, tell me do you know where your husband was yesterday?"

"He said he was here."

Oliver Hardy seemed to relax and looked at his colleague and nodded. "That is all for now but we will need to come back if we have any more questions. Your husband's situation is serious."

"When can I see him?"

"We will let you know."

Both Militia officers headed for the door. Snow gladly let them out.

Katya shook her head in despair and lit another cigarette. "I mean what the fuck? What is happening? What is this all about? Aidan do you understand anything?"

Snow put his arms around her. "Look you and I both know that Brian is harmless, he's a lover not a fighter."

Katya snorted. "He's not a lover either."

Snow ignored the insinuation. "At least we now know where he is. I'll go to the Embassy – I have contacts there and if they aren't going to charge him I'll get him out."

Katya started to cry. "Thank you Aidan. I'm scared. Can you stay here with me?"

Snow looked down at her. "I've got to see a few people but yes afterwards I'll come back and stay here. Get a pen and write down my number, just in case."

"OK." She smiled, reassured and moved away.

Snow had a thought. Brian and Katya's daughter was nowhere to be seen. "Where's Ana?"

"Summer camp." Katya replied, as she returned from the kitchen clutching a pen and a post-it note. She handed both to Snow who scribbled down his number. After he had finished there was a moment of silence. Katya spoke first. "Aidan I'm scared."

"I know, it's a scary thing to happen but wait here. Don't open the door or speak to anyone, I'll be back as soon as I can. Call me if you get worried or if anyone unexpected turns up. OK?"
"OK."
Snow kissed her on the forehead and left.

Volodymyrska Street, Kyiv

Alistair Vickers enjoyed relaxing in the bath. He had a CD of Bruch's Violin Concerto No. 1 in G minor playing as he luxuriated with a very expensive glass of Ukrainian Cognac. It was early Saturday evening and for once he had decided to cocoon himself from the world and its worries, his phone was off and he had no intention of answering the door. He found nowadays that he generally preferred his own company in his down time. Running with the 'Kyiv Hash House Harriers' or going to the ex-pat hang outs was fun but more and more it left him feeling empty. If he had been asked years ago where he would have seen himself at the age of forty five he would have said living in suburbia or some such foreign equivalent with a wife and two point four children yet here he was, single and inebriated sitting in a bath. Vickers smiled he mustn't get depressed, that had been a side effect of the painkillers he had previously become addicted to. No he must just relax and stop trying to explain his unbelievable lightness of being. He half smiled. Life was good, his life was good. Alistair Vickers was the SIS intelligence officer responsible for Ukraine. He closed his eyes but reminded himself that he mustn't fall asleep lest he become a second Whitney Houston.
He snapped his eyes open, the bath water was cold, the CD had ended and there was a ringing at his front door. He dragged his tired body out of the bath, pulled on a dark satin robe and made for the door. He peered through the spy-hole and couldn't believe who he was looking at.

HETMAN: DONETSK CALLING

Snow removed his finger from the bell as the door opened. He shook his head, for the second time that day he had been greeted by someone in a state of undress. "Alistair, you needn't have bothered getting dolled-up for me."

"Very droll. Come in."

Without being bid to do so Snow made for the kitchen and started to make himself a coffee. "I thought you would know I was here already?"

"On a work day maybe but my phone is off and so is my computer. So to what do I owe this unexpected pleasure?"

"Brian Webb is being held by the police."

Vickers sat at the kitchen table. "What for?"

Snow shrugged. "I don't know, the Militia wouldn't say."

"And how do you know this?"

"Coffee?"

"No I'm fine."

Snow added boiling water to his cup and stirred. "I was at his flat when the Militia came to question Katya." Snow sat and explained the events of the day thus far.

Vickers nodded. "If they haven't charged him they have to let him go, habeas corpus and all that. Unless the Militia has reason to believe it's related to terrorism."

"The only thing Brian terrorises are the local bars."

Vickers nodded at Snow's truism. Brian Webb was the largest ex-pat boozer possibly in the whole of Ukraine. His marriage to Katya had initially seemed to steady him somewhat. "You want me to go to the Militia station and petition for his release or at least get a clarification of his charges?"

"Alistair you are not just a pretty face."

Vickers shook his head. "Fine. Let me get a suit on and then you can tell me which regional station he's in."

"Thanks I owe you one."

"It's my job, just get me a bottle of the good stuff and we'll be even."

As Vickers left the room to dress, Snow went onto the balcony and looked at the street below. He missed Kyiv, he missed his old life but most of all he missed the friendships. For a tuppence ha'penny he'd quit the SIS and teach again. He'd happily swap his licence to kill for a contract to teach.
"Let's go." Vickers looked imposing in a dark blue Savile row suit, bespoke brogues and an 'old boy' public school tie.
Snow nodded his approval. "You scrub-up well for a dustman."
"Aidan as always I appreciate your honest feedback." He tossed Snow the keys to his diplomatic Land Rover defender. "You drive, I've had a few."

Berezniki Rayon, Kyiv

Snow parked the Land Rover Defender in front of the Berezniki Rayon Militia station and Vickers got out. They had decided that Snow would stay with the car, him potentially being seen by the same two officers who had questioned Katya earlier would raise questions. Snow opened a can of 'Burn' energy drink and observed life passing by.
Vickers entered the Militia station and was greeted by the desk officer berating an elderly woman. She was pleading with him to let her son go as he was innocent, but the officer would have none of it. In an angry voice and using no uncertain terms he told her to get lost. She left talking to herself. The desk officer looked up from his papers and was surprised to say the least to see Vickers standing in front of him. His mouth creased up a little as he asked, "Can I help?"
"Yes." Vickers answered in Ukrainian. Like Snow he was a fluent Russian speaker, unlike Snow he had also started to learn the real language of the country he lived in, Ukrainian. "My name is Alistair Vickers. I am the Commercial Attaché at the British Embassy and I believe you are holding a British Citizen without the due authority."

HETMAN: DONETSK CALLING

The Militia officer's mouth dropped open and he struggled for words. "Wh...What is the name of this Englishman?"

"Brian Webb."

The Ukrainian swallowed. "I see." He stared at his computer and wished it would engulf him. "He was here but he has now been transferred."

"What?" Vickers started to 'ham it up'. "Has Mr Webb been charged with anything?"

Again the Ukrainian looked, too hard, at his computer screen. "No. Not yet but he is being questioned in relation to a serious incident."

"Which is?"

"I'm sorry I can't say."

When Snow had approached Vickers earlier, Vickers had thought this all to be a commotion over nothing. A drunken episode perhaps that had done no harm but now he was starting to feel that something indeed was not as it should be. "So correct me if I am wrong. Mr Webb is being held, but not here for something that you say he may have been involved with but that same something you cannot confirm to me the nature of. Correct?"

The officer paused, confused. "Yes, that is so."

"So where is he now?"

The officer again checked his screen. "He is under the authority of Captain Budt."

"Now we are getting somewhere. Where is Captain Budt?"

"In transit with the prisoner."

"But Mr Webb has not been charged."

"But sexual assault is a serious matter."

"So are you confirming to me that Mr Brian Webb is being accused of sexual assault?"

The Militia officer had been forced into a corner and had made a mistake. "No, not at this time but perhaps."

"So where is Mr Webb in transit to?"

"I am sorry I cannot say."

"What is your name officer?"

"Brovchenko, Yuri."

"Well Officer Brovchenko, first thing on Monday morning if Mr Webb does not reappear or is released I shall be lodging a complaint with the head of the city Militia and the Ministry of Internal Affairs. Am I making myself understood, Yuri?"

Brovchenko nodded. "Yes."

"Good. Goodbye."

Snow watched Vickers leave the Militia station and was irked to see he was alone. Vickers climbed into the Land Rover, the look on his face showed confusion. Snow asked. "Where's Brian?"

"That's the thing, they won't tell me."

"What? I don't get it?"

"Drive and I'll explain."

Snow shook his head after Vickers repeated the conversation and said. "Have you ever heard of this happening before?"

"Never. That is what's so strange. He is guaranteed access to a representative from the Embassy yet we weren't informed and now he is moved without being charged?" Vickers massaged the bridge of his nose between his thumb and forefinger. He had the start of a headache. "There's nothing more I can do until Monday morning. Where are you staying?"

"At Brian's flat with Katya."

Vickers removed his hand from his face and looked at Snow. "Isn't she that sexy one with the..."

"Yes and she is also my friend's wife."

"Good, just as long as you remember."

Snow rolled his eyes. "Who do you take me for – Mitch Turney?"

"No." Vickers laughed. Their mutual friend had a well-deserved reputation as a womaniser. "Are you going to give him a call?"

"I should, and Michael Jones. They may have been with him yesterday."

HETMAN: DONETSK CALLING

The two SIS operatives arrived back at Vickers' apartment building. Unlike Webb's 1980's monstrosity on the city's left bank, this building had architectural worth and character. All its occupants were expatriates. Snow turned off the engine and handed Vickers the keys. "So I'll call you first thing on Monday?"

"Agreed."

"Thanks."

They got out of the car.

"Aidan, if he is implicated in sexual assault then you know we both have to distance ourselves from him don't you?"

"I know, but he's not."

"I just 'know of' him but you 'know him' so I'll bow to your better judgement." Vickers waved and entered his building.

Khreshatik Street, Kyiv

Snow headed for Kyiv's main shopping street Khreshatik and his meeting with Michael Jones. Jones had been only too happy to get away from his wife Inna and catch up with his old drinking partner. As Snow walked he suddenly realised that he had not eaten since 'lunch' on the aeroplane some hours before or indeed had much to drink. Although it was evening the temperature was still in the high twenties, a whole fifteen degrees higher than it had been on Worthing's seafront that same morning. Snow used the underpass to cross from one side of the wide street to the other and then entered the large McDonalds that stood on top of the Metro station. It had been Jones' choice of meeting place. Even after years in Ukraine the Welshman remained fussy about what he ate unless he'd cooked it himself. The eatery was fairly busy with a few families but mostly twenty and thirty-somethings chatting and flirting or taking advantage of the free Wi-Fi. A figure waved from a large semi-circular seat. Snow couldn't help but smile at seeing his old friend. Michael Jones had not changed a bit. With his craggy features and dark blonde hair he looked like 'the drinking mans' Gordon Ramsey.

"Aidan, Hokay?" The Welshman's accent caused a couple of diners to stare.

Snow adopted a fake Welsh accent. "Hello Mister Jones, how are you?"

"Eh, not bad." Jones beamed. "Just look at the crumpet in here!"

They sat and Snow laughed out loud. Jones had never been subtle. "It's good to see you Michael."

"You too. It's been far too long. You teaching again?"

Jones knew of Snow's Military past, that he had been a member of the SAS and of course the events that had led to their mutual friend, Arnaud's death. Jones did not however know that since then Snow had been recruited into the Secret Intelligence Service. Snow decided to stick with his legend. "I'm teaching at a private school near Knightsbridge."

"Full of Arabs I bet."

"Not politically correct, but correct."

Jones raised his eyebrows and the tone of his voice to express mock outrage. "Politically incorrect? Politically incorrect! As a native Welsh speaker, I'm an ethnic minority myself!"

It was good to see his friend again but he had to move things on.

Michael sensed Snow had become serious. "So what's all this about Brian?"

"He called me this morning asking for help, I got here to find he's being held by the police for sexual assault."

"Brian? Sexual assault? GBH – grievous beer harm I could envisage but sexual assault?" Jones' Welsh intonation rose at the end.

"Only that's not all." Snow explained the visit to the Militia station.

"So where is he?"

Snow shrugged. "They won't say just that he is the custody of an officer named Budt."

"It's the bandits from Donetsk, mark my words."

"When was the last time you saw him?"

"Yesterday. We started off in the Dockers Pub – you know the new name for 'The Cowboy Bar' and then onto Arena."

"And nothing happened?"

Jones shook his head. "Mitch was with us but he went home with a tart from his office. Inna ordered me to come home and the last I saw of Brian he was getting into a taxi."

"What time was this?"

Jones frowned. "Dunno, maybe three-ish? You know how it is."

Snow nodded. In his day the drinking sessions usually ended in the small hours. "Is Mitch around?"

"No, he flew back to the US this morning to see his kids and ex-wife."

Snow felt his stomach rumble and stole a fry from Jones' tray. "None of this makes sense."

"Correction, none of it would make sense in the UK. Here it makes perfect sense; someone is after a 'Vziatka'."

"A bribe?" Something clicked in Snow's mind and things became a little clearer.

"For sure. Look at the time I got stopped without my passport back in the days when you needed a visa. Even though I had a photocopy on me they wanted $100. The next day they came to the flat and saw Inna. She told them to piss off because she knew their boss."

"I hope you're right Michael. But we still have to find out where he is." Snow felt his Blackberry vibrate. He retrieved it from his pocket and looked at the number displayed. It was Brian's flat. "Katya?"

"Aidan, the Militia came back – I pretended not to be in. They were banging the door."

"I'm on my way."

Her voice almost broke as she asked. "Is Brian with you?"

"No. I'm sorry; I'll explain when I see you." He ended the call and looked at Jones. "Gotta go."

Snow stood at the side of the road and stretched his arm out. A beat-up Volkswagen saloon immediately swung in from the early evening traffic and came to an abrupt stop in front of him. As was the custom and common practice, it wasn't a taxi just a Kyivite taking the chance to make bit extra. Snow gave the driver the address and in return the driver stated an inflated price. Snow was in no mood to haggle, agreed the price instantly and jumped in. Twenty minutes later he was once more outside Webb's building; he called Katya again and let her know that he was on his way up. Two minutes after that she opened the door and ushered him in.
"Are you Ok?" He asked.
She nodded and looked over his shoulder expectantly. "Where's Brian?"
"I don't know. The Militia have moved him. Let's get inside."
She shut the door and bolted it. "Where is my husband?"
"I don't know. They wouldn't say but my friend at the Embassy has threatened to make an official complaint if Brian is not released or charged by Monday."
Katya folded her arms, and prepared herself for the worst. "What are they going to charge him with?"
"Let's sit down first."
"Bollocks, Aidan just tell me. Please."
"Sexual assault."
Katya backed away into the kitchen and raised her hand to her mouth, stifling a laugh. Snow couldn't tell if it was nerves or if she actually found it funny. "He can barely assault me."
"Tell me what happened here, with the Militia?"
"The same two officers came back. They rang the bell and when I didn't answer said they knew I was in. They then banged on the door for a few minutes and said that I couldn't help Brian if

I didn't let them in. Aidan I thought they were going to break the door down."

"I doubt that they would have done that. You did the right thing."

"Are you hungry?"

Snow was but didn't want to make her cook. "If you're going to eat then I will."

"Stop being so bloody English." Katya pointed at a chair. "Sit. Eat. And take your shoes off."

Snow looked down, first at his trainers and then at a bowl of Borsch that had been awaiting his arrival. "Thanks and sorry."

She sat opposite him and held her hands together tightly. "Aidan I'm scared."

"Katya, I think I know why they have Brian, well sort of."

"I don't understand. What do you mean?"

"Well we both know that Brian wouldn't sexually assault anyone so what are they holding him for? A bribe. Think about it. He's got his own company, Ok he lives here but I know he's worth a bit. Or at least he used to be."

"What's wrong with my flat?"

"It's very nice."

"Aidan I know it's shit so don't try and put spaghetti on my ears." She pushed a plastic pot towards him. "Smetana?"

"Thanks." Snow ladled the sour cream into his soup. "So someone has been watching and has decided that Brian needs to pay to operate here."

"Then they have chosen the wrong person. Brian has never once paid for a Krisha, and he won't start now."

Snow ate his soup and thought in silence. The Krisha Katya referred to was the 'roof' the protection offered by one mafia gang against attacks or threats by others and in some cases the Militia and tax police. "Well this is the most logical answer, unless of course it's a misunderstanding or a case of mistaken identity."

"Or he's guilty." Katya managed a smile. "Which he's not. So what can we do now?"

"We have until Monday for official channels to do anything but I think that we'll be contacted before that with a demand."

Katya frowned and shook her head. "Doesn't this mean he's been kidnapped?"

Snow hadn't thought about it like that. "That's one way of looking at it." He finished his borsch and pushed the plate away.

"More?"

"No, I'm full."

Katya stood, collected her cigarettes and moved onto the balcony. Snow washed his plate and spoon in the sink then joined her. The view of the city was quite something and worth more than the flat itself. It was one of only a few flats in the complex that still retained an unobstructed sightline to the river and the distant city beyond. As the summer evening gently lost its light the air seemed to glow with both the heat of the day and the myriad of windows.

"Screw me."

"What?"

"Aidan, I want you to screw me." She reached for his belt.

"Katya stop." He placed his hands over hers.

"Don't you want to?"

"How can I answer that?"

"Don't you fancy me?"

"Of course I do, I always have."

"But?"

"You are the wife of one of my closest friends."

"Just because I want to have sex with you does not mean that I don't love Brian. And besides he'll never know."

"But I will." He looked into her eyes, she raised her eyebrow suggestively. "No. I'm sorry and believe me I'm regretting turning you down already."

"You really are a Knight in Shining armour coming to the rescue?"
"Yes and my lance is staying locked up."
She laughed and pulled her hands away. "Tart."
"What?"
"I have some tart, would you like some?" Before Snow could answer the doorbell rang and then there was the sound of heavy banging. "It's them."
"OK talk to them through the peep-hole, I'll stand by your side. Then we'll decide what to do. Agreed?"
"Agreed."
They moved towards the front door as the ringing and banging continued, now joined by the sound of; "Militia open the door".
"What do you want?" Katya asked.
"Open the door. We have some questions that you need to answer. It will help your husband." It was Oliver Hardy. "You surely don't want us to conduct our business on the doorstep? Do you want your neighbours to know what you husband had done?"
Snow touched Katya's arm. "Let them in. I'll wait behind the door in the kitchen. I'll be ready if you need me."
"But Aidan they may hurt me."
"If they do I'll kill them."
Katya looked at Snow and saw on his face an expression she hadn't seen before. "OK."
Outside the officer shouted again. "Come one now Madam Webb, let us in so we can discuss the criminal activity of your husband."
She took a deep breath and opened the door. "Come in."
Oliver Hardy leered at her and walked directly into the lounge whilst Stan Laurel removed his cap and smiled weakly. They both sat on the settee. Katya remained standing, arms folded.
"What kind of hospitality is this? You have not offered us a drink!" The older officer barked. Katya could tell he'd been drinking. Snow could hear it in his voice too and knew it would

make him volatile but slow. "Even your homosexual American friend who was here earlier offered me tea."

"He was English and he has manners."

"I am sure. So officer Brovchenko explain to Madam Webb here the situation."

Stan Laurel swallowed hard and readied himself. "We received a report from a young lady who stated that your husband made unwarranted sexual advances to her last night. When she told him to stop he attempted to..." Brovchenko started to blush.

"Go on." Goaded Hardy.

"Your husband grabbed the woman and tried to have sex with her against a wall."

Katya burst out laughing. "With his bad knee? My husband is very overweight and almost fifty six. Let me tell you that his days of athletic fucking are long gone!"

"I think you should watch your language."

"And I think you should bring my husband to me and stop being a disgrace to your uniform! And another thing, try speaking Ukrainian both of you!"

Hardy fought to restrain himself. "Enough. You will listen to officer Brovchenko or things will only get worse!"

"Please go ahead, I like fairy tales."

Brovchenko frowned. Things were not going as planned. "There is no doubt from the evidence that your husband is guilty and he would be found as such by any judge. But there may be something we can do, to help."

From his hiding place Snow was praying that Katya would not provoke them anymore. All she really had to do was to listen. And that gave Snow an idea. He switched on the audio record function on his Blackberry, carefully reached around the kitchen door and placed it on the floor in the lounge.

Brovchenko looked at his colleague. "Officer Klyuyvets shall I...?"

Klyuyvets held up his hand. "What my young friend is attempting to say is that the lady, the innocent victim of your

husband's unprovoked attack is willing to drop all charges, withdraw her sworn statement for financial compensation. You understand she is a student from a good family and any publicity, while she is blameless would tarnish her reputation."
"How much?" Katya asked.
"I believe that she would accept $75,000."
"And what guarantee do I have that this goes no further?"
Klyuyvets put his hand to his heart in mock surprise. "My word, our word officer Brovchenko and I."
"And if we pay $80,000 can my husband fuck her?"
Snow sighed. Katya was playing with fire.
Klyuyvets pulled himself to his feet. "Do you think this is some kind of a joke? This is a serious matter."
"It would be best for your husband and his business interests if you were to pay." Added Brovchenko.
There was a ringing. Snow cursed silently. It was his Blackberry. Katya moved to collect it.
"Is someone else here?" Klyuyvets snapped.
Snow decided the time for playing hide and seek was over and stepped into the lounge.
"You again."
"I think you should tell Mrs Webb where her husband is before I force it out of you."
Klyuyvets almost fell over. "He speaks Russian and insults two officers of the law!"
Snow took a step forward. "Where is Brian Webb?"
"Hold out your hands, I will cuff you and take you to him. You are under arrest for attempting to assault two Militia officers."
Brovchenko started to unclip his cuffs. "Please give me your wrists."
"Because your own are limp?"
Brovchenko frowned the true meaning of the idiom did not translate from English to Russian. "No, I need to put handcuffs on you."

Without warning Klyuyvets lunged at Snow, swinging his arm. Snow adjusted his stance and stepped aside. The fat man's face contorted with rage and he reached for his baton. Without hesitation Snow grabbed the officer's arm turned his wrist and using a pressure hold pinned him to the floor. Klyuyvets grunted and struggled. Brovchenko gawped and then reached for his pistol. Snow sprang up and with one hand pushed the trigger arm sideways whilst the other landed a punch on his jaw. The thin officer stumbled backwards and then collapsed. His head hit the floor with a heavy thud rendering him unconscious. Snow turned the older man was now on his knees.
"You piece of shit!" Klyuyvets swung his baton at Snow, who stepped out of the way and kicked the officer in the head which snapped back rendering him too unconscious.
"Aidan, what have you done?" Katya put her hands on her head.
He ignored Katya's question and checked both men were still breathing and that their skulls were not fractured before cuffing them with own cuffs. "At least we now know what they wanted. Check their ID."
Still in a mild state of shock she did as she was told. "Ah, that's why they refused to speak Ukrainian." She pointed to a driving licence. "They are from Donetsk."
"Makes sense, new faces come in and want their share of the 'cake'."
Katya nodded and started to rant. "Since that goat became president he's been replacing everyone with his own people. My friend's an estate agent and she says that most of the companies renovating flats are from the East, especially the Donbas region. On the roads there are more and more cars with number plates starting with 'AN' – Donetsk and can you believe this even the supermarkets are using Eastern Ukrainian suppliers! The country is going down the toilet!"
Snow knew all of this, but did not interrupt her, she needed to talk, to vent - it would help lessen her shock. Most of Russian

speaking population of Ukraine wanted closer ties with Russian now that their man had become President and the last vestige of the Orange Revolution had been swept away. 'Party' men from the East had come to the capital and started what was at first called a 'quiet coup'. Now however more and more noise was being made as they continued to gain control of public and private bodies.

Katya continued. "That's why we are going to move. I've been offered a job in London. My bank's re-launching its Eastern European venture capital unit. They want me to be part of the team dealing with Ukraine and Russia."

"So you'll be speaking Russian and dealing with the 'Bandits from Donetsk'."

"Oh shit." Her focus turned again to the two recumbent officers. "Oh shit Aidan, what have you done?"

"I saw red, I hate bullies." Snow realised he had made a mistake but it had felt good to slap the two men silly.

"But they'll be missed, we'll get arrested!"

Snow looked at his phone. "Maybe not, we've got some leverage. Tell me about your neighbours?"

"But why..."

"Please."

She frowned. "That side," she pointed to the left, "is owned by an old woman. She never speaks to me. She's half deaf, keeps herself to herself."

"So she probably wouldn't have heard anything."

"And the flat across from us is owned by an alcoholic."

"A fiend of Brian's?"

"Ha ha. No. He's very loud when he's pissed."

"So we can assume that if anyone did hear anything they may think it was the bloke across the hall?"

"Ok, I get it. But what happens when the Militia come looking for them?"

"Hopefully we won't need to keep hold of them for that long."

"Aidan, I don't like any of this. This is my home and now I've got two bound up policemen in the middle of my lounge."

"Then we'll move them."

"Great. Where to?"

"The bathroom."

"I thought you meant somewhere else? Somewhere outside."

"Can you get me your ironing board, duck-tape and any spare belts of Brian's?"

Katya cast him an odd look. "Have you been reading Fifty Shades of Grey?"

"Just do it."

Whilst Katya moved into the bedroom to look for belts, Snow dragged the diminutive Officer Brovchenko into the bathroom where he removed the man's shoes. Katya showed him where the ironing board was and Snow placed it under the still comatose officer. The man's shackled arms were behind him and underneath the board. Katya handed him two belts. Snow nodded in approval. Made for a man with a huge waist they easily went around the thin officer twice and secured him to the board. Katya looked on none the wiser whilst Snow searched the bathroom.

"Is this your face cloth?" He asked her.

"Yes but it needs to be washed."

"All the better. Katya. I need you to go and sit in the lounge and keep watch over 'Mr Angry'."

"What are you going to do?"

"You don't want to see what I'm going to do."

"Who are you Aidan, I mean really?"

"A friend. Now go into the lounge."

Snow removed his polo-shirt then manoeuvred Brovchenko so that the board was leaning against the bath like a see-saw. The board creaked slightly, it wouldn't hold for long but was all he had available. He then gently lowered the end with the officers' head into the bath before turning on the shower. The icy cold water splashed onto the Ukrainian's face; his feet began to tap and his eyes shot open. As the water travelled into his mouth and up his nose he started to splutter and choke. Snow pushed down and the man's head came clear of the water. He coughed and then fought for air. Water-Boarding was an extreme measure but Snow was in a hurry. He still however hoped that he would not have to take it too far. Snow started his questioning without wasting any more time. "Where is Brian Webb?"

"I don't know...let me go." Brovchenko spluttered.

Snow placed the wet facecloth over the man's face and then let his head drop down again into the shower. This time the material clung to his face, making it more difficult for air to get into his nostrils and mouth. Brovchenko felt as though he was drowning. He pulled his arms and tried to kick with his feet as his panic increased. It was at this point that he emptied his bladder. Snow pulled him up again and removed the towel.

"Where is Brian Webb?"

"You can't do this to me I'm a serving Militia officer! You'll be thrown in jail!"

Snow slowly draped the facecloth once more on the young officer's face as he did so the man started to talk – the words muffled. Snow removed the cloth. "Where is Webb?"

"I've got a Krisha! I'm protected by..." His words were cut short by the facecloth once more.

Snow held him under longer this time before snapping him upright. He wasn't sure how long the home-made device would last so he had to increase the risk. "Now tell me where is Webb?"

Gasping for air Brovchenko replied. "He's at a house in Petropavlivska Borschagivka."

"Not a Militia station?"

"No."

"Where exactly? What's the address?"

"It's in Meer Street...26. Yes Meer 26. Now please let me go."

'Meer' the Russian for 'peace'. The fact that Brian was being held at a private house and not an official address confirmed to him without a doubt that this was all a rouse. "Who provides your Krisha?"

Officer Brovchenko became wide eyed as he realised the full cost of his error. "No I can't!"

Snow slapped him in the face with his open palm, replaced the face cloth and dunked his face again. This time he held him for as long as he dared before tipping him back up. It took a whole thirty seconds for Brovchenko to recover enough to be able to speak. "Ruslan Imyets." The name meant nothing to Snow and Brovchenko noticed this fact with shock. "Ruslan Imyets is a Verhovna Rada Deputy with the Party of Regions for Donbas."

Snow nodded satisfied that he'd got all he needed. "Officer Brovchenko, were you responsible for the abduction of Brian Webb?"

Brovchenko saw a way out. "No. There were others involved."

Snow nodded, the man had taken the bait. "Your group has made a serious error in kidnapping Mr Webb and attempting blackmail his wife. Now I understand that you perhaps are naïve enough to have been caught up in this, coerced into becoming part of this criminal group."

"Yes that's what happened."

"So in that case I can offer you a deal."

For the second time that evening Snow was asked "Who are you?"

"I am the person who if he wished could drown you here like a rat but I'm giving you the chance of a clean break."

Obolon Rayon, Kyiv

An odd buzzing awoke the Ukrainian from a much needed sleep. He picked up his mobile and looked at the screen. The number was withheld. The average person may have ignored

the call or let it go to voicemail but Vitaly Blazhevich was not an average person and his number was anything but public. The Ukrainian Intelligence Service (SBU) anti-corruption & organised crime operative pressed the accept button. "Allo?" His voice was thick from sleep and his mind still dulled but this instantly changed when he heard the English voice at the other end. "Aidan, where are you?"
"Left bank."
"Kyiv's left bank?"
"I'm not in Paris if that's what you mean."
Blazhevich sat up, looked at his clock and shook his head. It was just after midnight, he'd been in bed for forty minutes. His wife groaned next to him and he wisely decided to leave the room to continue the call. The last time Blazhevich and Snow had 'worked' together they had prevented a terrorist attack. "Ok so I guess it's important?"
"Important and personal."
"Let me have it." Blazhevich padded to the kitchen, poured a glass of water and then entered his own balcony. A new high-rise development in Kyiv's Obolon district it too had a river view. He sat on a plastic chair as Snow re-counted the day's events.
"Well?" Snow asked.
"Aidan you have an uncanny knack of walking into things. There is an on-going investigation into Deputy Imyets. If we can implicate him in this then I am sure even Dudka would be happy."
"How is the old man?" Snow had a soft spot for the elderly SBU Director.
"Grumpy."
Both men chuckled.
"So when can I expect you?"
"I'll be there in half an hour." Blazhevich replied.

ALEX SHAW

Levo Berezna, Kyiv

Officers Brovchenko and Klyuyev were both gagged. Brovchenko stank of his own urine whilst Klyuyev stank of alcohol and fear. Snow had taken great pleasure in informing the senior officer that their operation was blown and that they were now the ones in trouble. Neither of the Ukrainians knew quite what to expect but when Vitaly Blazhevich arrived it certainly was not the SBU. Both had watched in shock as the newcomer had identified himself to Webb's wife as a member of the SBU's Main Directorate for Combating Corruption and Organized Crime and then joked with the Englishman. They then felt their hearts sink even more when the Englishman produced a recording of their attempts at extortion. Although inadmissible, as all audio recordings were in Ukrainian courts, it could be leaked to the press and posted on the internet. In short unless they co-operated fully they either faced lengthy jail sentences or ran the risk of being 'taken care of' by their own group.
"I've checked the address you gave me. I thought it sounded familiar and as you would say it has 'come up trumps'."
"How?"
"It is the address of Ruslan Imyets' new Kyiv 'dacha'. If that is indeed where Mr Webb is being held then I cannot see how Deputy Imyets can deny his involvement."
Katya had been sitting in silence and starring at the two Militia officers. She was one to hold a grudge and whilst Snow had been wondering if his interrogation technique had been too much she had told him it had been too little. Brovchenko had of course been the weaker of the two officers but that pig Klyuyev had deserved to be drowned. She looked across at Blazhevich, a man who she had not met before but who seemed to be very friendly with Snow and asked. "When do we go and get Brian?"
"I shall have to ask my Director but there are two possible scenarios that come to mind. The first is that we get a warrant to

search the address – but this will tip off Imyets, the second is that we wait until Vickers has gone through his official channels. This is of course on the provision that Mr Webb is not released."

"What about the third option?"

Blazhevich fixed Snow with a hard stare. "I know that it hasn't stopped you before, but you are not here in an official capacity remember? We have an on-going investigation which we must not jeopardise."

"So," Katya asked again, "when do we go and get Brian."

***

Snow sipped his coffee as Katya moved around the kitchen making breakfast. In the night an SBU team had arrived to take the Laurel and Hardy into custody. Snow and Katya had been left alone. They had shared the same bed but she had not made any more advances towards him and he was glad that his resolve had not been tested further. She was a beautiful woman, doubtless a great mother and propositions aside a good wife. Inside he felt a pang of jealousy for the normal life that he couldn't have.

"Are you starring at my bum?"

Snow was. "Yes but I was thinking about something else."

"Charming. Here's your omelette."

"Thanks." He waited for her to sit and then ate in silence before speaking again. "Look, I know what Vitaly said about his department's investigation but the longer Brian is held the higher the risk is that he may get hurt."

"I agree."

"So I'm going to check out the house myself."

"Aidan you are not Rambo and besides didn't Vitaly say they had an observation post set up nearby?"

"Katya, I can't just sit here and do nothing. Vitaly is good at his job, his boss Director Dudka is a legend but the SBU is a state apparatus and as such by definition ponderous and prone to leaks."

There was a silence as Snow ate. Katya broke it. "Aidan you really are a good friend. I feel bad that Brian and I weren't here for you when your friend Arnaud was killed."

Snow shrugged. "Thanks, but you were both in Odessa at the time, trying to make a go of it."

"And look where it got us four years later."

"I still think it's a nice flat."

"I still think you are at times too English."

The bell at the front door chirped.

"That'll be Vitaly." Snow answered the door and Blazhevich entered.

"So I've spoken to Dudka."

"How is he?"

"Even though you are the reason I had to get him out of bed, he is happy you are not yet dead Aidan. He asks that you call Vickers and tell him to hold off with his 'complaint'. He says that we must preserve the investigation until we have 100% positive proof that Brian Webb is at the house. And then he says we can by all means 'storm the place'."

"That sounds like Dudka."

Katya glanced at Snow then at Blazhevich. "So can't you just take a photograph of Brian through a window?"

"Yes, if he is near or passes by a window."

"Oh." She frowned.

"So apart from 'eyes on' I'm at a loss."

"Get me inside."

"How?"

"You said it was Deputy Imyets new 'dacha'?"

"Yes."

"Well is it new or did someone live there before?"

"I'll find out."

"Good. If there was a previous owner then I become their 'drunken' ex-pat friend who's come over for a drink."
Blazhevich looked at Snow with a strange expression. "You don't just think out of the box, you dispense with it."
"Is that a complement?"
"An observation."
"Hm, boxing clever."

Petropavlivska Borschagivka village, Kyiv Oblast

The observation post was in a partly built church almost opposite the target building. Snow had passed the church many times over the years as his American pal Mitch Turney lived a few streets along. A two man SBU team had kept a vigil on the target overnight and were happy to be relieved by Blazhevich and Snow. Blazhevich had found out that the house was nine years old and the last person to live in it had been a German by the name of Eric. Snow laughed at this but Blazhevich did not see the humour. After again discussing it with Dudka, who now was also at his own dacha away from the Ukrainian capital city, Snow's plan had been officially agreed upon. Snow would approach the house, feigning inebriation and see what he could find out. In Snow's mind he either caught a glimpse of Brian or he didn't either way he saw no risk, at least this is what he had told his friends in the SBU. Snow however had other ideas as to what may happen. Whilst they waited until a reasonable hour for Snow to make his approach, Blazhevich and Snow reviewed the surveillance tapes of the day before. When they reached ten a.m. a lumbering overweight figure could be seen being taken into the house but unfortunately his face had been pointing away from the camera. Snow was sure it was Brian but Blazhevich shrugged, he didn't know him.
"Time to go." Snow checked his watch it was almost midday. Blazhevich nodded. "No heroics just see what you can see."

Snow smiled. "I'm not a hero." He shuffled away from the window to the back of the church and opened a bottle of beer. He took a swig and poured the rest into his hand and rubbed it over his face, letting some run onto his day-old polo-shirt. He then picked up two bottles of whiskey and left the church by the rear exit. He walked into the woods behind turned right and found a path; it brought him back to the street but further up the road and around a bend, out of direct line of sight of the target address. He started to walk and as he did so he made sure to adjust to gait to that of someone who clearly had been drinking. As he rounded a bend he saw the house and immediately crossed the road, heading directly towards it. The house faced the road and had a two meter high brick wall surrounding it. There were no signs of exterior security except for the large ornate metal gate that acted as an entrance. The house itself was three stories tall and was built of red brick. In comparison to the other overtly ornate or ugly houses surrounding it, the target seemed quite tasteful. Snow rang the doorbell then stared into the small camera he now saw mounted slightly above.
There was a pause and then a voice asked in Russian. "What do you want?"
Snow started to prepare his Oscar acceptance speech. "Eric you wanker! I'm back in town and I've brought two friends!" Snow held up the bottles to the camera. "Come on you German Gay-Lord open the door and let's get drinking!"
There was a hiss of static before a voice answered in faltering English. "Eric no here. You go."
Snow needed to get into the house, he'd see nothing otherwise. "Eric open the door and stop being a poof! Come on, my two friends here are getting impatient!"
There was a slight buzzing sound and a click. The gate opened and Snow stepped inside. It was closed behind him by a large figure in a black t-shirt and urban combat trousers. He looked at Snow then pointed to the front door. Snow surreptitiously

looked around. He was standing in a large paved courtyard. The house was directly ahead; to the left was a slope which led down to the underground garage. Past this he could see a lush green lawn. Directly to his right was a fountain and small 'dacha style' out-house. The front door opened and two uniformed Militia officers greeted him.

Snow smiled. "Is Eric having a party?"

"Who you are?" The first asked in English. Snow realised it was the same voice he had heard on the telephone the day before.

"I'm a friend of Eric. Who are you?" Snow replied and placed his bottles on the step.

"My name is Officer Kopylenko and you are very drunk."

Snow raised his arms smiling. "Guilty as charged!"

Kopylenko pointed at him. "Tell me please, what is your name?"

Snow gave his own name; he had no reason to lie. "Aidan Snow. Nice to meet you."

"Can I see your passport Mr Snow?"

"I'm sorry; I don't have it with me."

"Hm, I see. In that case I am very sorry but I shall have to issue you with a fine."

Snow pointed at the bottles. "Is there not something else I could give you?"

"We will take those too, but you must pay a fine."

"Fine, that's fine!" Snow started to laugh and retrieved a wad of notes from his pocket. As he did so he made sure that it slipped through his fingers and fell on the ground. He noticed Kopylenko eye-up the bundle of bills greedily. Snow shakily retrieved the money and smiled. "Now officer, how much do I need to give you? Will $100 be enough?" As Snow held out the notes he looked around. "Where is Eric?"

"I told you Eric is not here. This is the wrong house. Give me all your money and you can go."

Snow made a decision, double or nothing. "Where is Eric? Are you robbing him?" He tried to push past the two men but the second officer grabbed his arm. Snow half-heartedly punched him in the face before shouting, "Eric I'm on my way!" The officer loosened his grip and Snow burst into the house only to be pushed to the floor a moment later. Several heavy kicks connected with Snow's torso and as he was dragged to his feet a fist hit him in the side of the head causing him to see stars.

Kopylenko spoke again. "You have assaulted a Militia officer. We now must arrest you and keep you here until you are processed."

"Let me go. I'm a British citizen!" Snow protested.

Kopylenko spoke the second officer in Russian. "Take him away and put him with the other English idiot."

Snow let his feet drag and his head loll forward as the officer moved him down a flight of stairs and then pushed him into another room. The heavy door was locked behind him. Snow rubbed his head and looked around. It was a wine cellar but empty apart from the racks. There was a narrow barred window to one side at head height which let in the only source of light through which he could see a flower bed.

"Bloody Hell! Aidan you found me!"

Snow noticed a large dishevelled figure sitting on a patio chair. "Hello Brian."

Webb smiled. "How the heck did you get here?"

"Connections."

"Aidan thanks a million for coming."

Snow held his forefinger to his mouth, then moved back to the door and listened. He could hear nothing through it. He nodded at Webb. "Tell me what happened?"

"I was out with Mitch and Michael having a few – you know how it is, and then got a taxi home. The driver stopped the car, I thought he needed a piss but then he just 'legged it'. Then when I got out to see where the heck he was going some blokes came at me. I thought it was a bloody team of hit-men! Aidan, I was that tanked-up that I just got back in the taxi and drove off. I tried to lose them but crashed into a sodding bus shelter, shook me up I can tell you." Webb lifted his grey fringe to show his blooded forehead. "I kept moving until I couldn't go any further. Then I called you."

"And they grabbed you."

"Yep. I was that blotto and shagged out that I couldn't do anything to stop them. They slapped me around a bit for good measure."

One against four was bad enough odds for anyone but an overweight drunk pushing sixty had no chance. "The Militia came to see Katya."

"How is she? Is she ok?" Webb's face showed real concern.

"She's fine. She told the Militia to go screw themselves. They said that unless she paid them $75000 they were going to charge you with sexual assault."

Webb burst out laughing. "On whom, me self?"

"They say you grabbed a woman and tried to shag her up against a wall."

"If only." Webb stood, hobbled towards Snow and hugged him. "Thanks again for coming, I knew you would."

"What are friends for? Brian don't worry, I've spoken to the SBU. They are building a case against the bloke these goons report to."

"So who you are working for now, MI6?"

"It's called the Secret Intelligence Service nowadays, but yes."

"Does your watch become a power boat?"

Snow found another chair and sat. "You really can be a silly sod, do you know that?"

Webb nodded. "So the SBU are investigating Katya's ex-husband?"

"Her 'ex' is a Politician?"

"No, he's the Militia thug running this, Pavel Kopylenko."

Snow frowned. "He's Ana's father?"

"Yes. He's the reason I'm here."

"I don't understand."

"Aidan. Katya's been offered a great job in London. But as Ana is underage we need her father's written consent for her to leave the country."

"Which I assume he had refused?"

"You assume right. So, Katya and I have had to start legal proceedings to attempt to get a court ruling stating that we can take Ana to the UK."

"And he's trying to stop this?"

"That's why I called you Aidan. Katya doesn't know about this, but first he went after my business and now he's going after me. Shit, if I get framed for sexual assault no judge in their right mind will grant me custody over him for Ana." Webb put his head in his hands and it was several seconds before he spoke again. "I'm her dad, not him".

"What exactly has Kopylenko said to you?"

"He never said anything about sexual assault the crafty bastard; I thought it was all about my joy-ride in the taxi. He said on Monday they are going to present me and their 'evidence' to the judge. Kopylenko said unless they receive payment from Katya the judge will have no option but to find me guilty. So who's this politician bloke the SBU are after?"

"The owner of this house, Ruslan Imyets."

Webb rolled his eyes and let out a humourless laugh. "Imyets, the Verhovna Rada Deputy? I should be honoured."

"You know him?"

"I've heard of him, he's in pharmaceuticals, before that he was Militia officer. The channel TVi ran a story on him, it very nearly put them out of business. He's one of the most aggressive bandits from Donetsk, one of the President's own 'Donbas business buddies'. In the last two years Imyets has won more tenders than anyone else, and he's used some very unsavoury means to secure them. Heck, if Kopylenko's working for Imyets he's got some serious Krisha!"

Snow thought for a moment. "What's the connection between Kopylenko and Imyets?"

HETMAN: DONETSK CALLING

"Kopylenko is a Militia officer from Donetsk. Apart from that I don't know."

"Have you ever had any dealings with Imyets?"

"No, we don't move in quite the same circles."

Snow stretched out and fell his ribs. He'd just have a few bruises. "You know I don't think Imyets knows anything about this. No offence Brian, but why would he bother with you?"

"I agree. I just sell books, not even mucky ones. I could murder a drink." Webb raised his arms and gestured around the room. "Ironic eh, they put me in an empty wine cellar."

Blazhevich checked his watch again. What was taking Snow so long? He cursed. He knew the Englishman too well, he'd 'improvised'. There was a buzzing next to him and he picked up Snow's Blackberry which the SIS operative had intentionally left behind. "Hello Alistair."

"Vitaly, this means Snow is with you?"

"He was but now he's checking out the address where we believe Webb is being held. I've got an eyeball on the location."

"Which Militia station are they in?"

"They are not. It's a private house belonging to Ruslan Imyets. They are holding him hostage."

"So the kidnappers are Militia officers in the pocket of Ruslan Imyets?"

"Correct, which is why Dudka wanted you to back off."

"Understood." Vickers was annoyed it was all happening without him. "So what is Aidan doing?"

"He is inside looking for Brian. We had a plan; Aidan's a drunk ex-pat looking up an old friend."

"I see. So now they've got two hostages?"

"It looks that way."

"So the plan is working Vitaly?"

Blazhevich shook his head. Both Vickers and Snow always thought they knew best, even though they had very different approaches. "Yes. If it was not the correct location they would have sent Aidan 'packing', but if we presume they are holding him then all we do is wait until he is moved."

In his flat Vickers sipped his tea. "So what would the SBU like me to do?"

"We need to get something on Imyets. The SBU cannot 'go in' unless there is evidence of his involvement that'll hold up in court otherwise our entire investigation will be blown. I can watch but I can't act."

"OK. I'll wait until Monday lunchtime and then if we don't have Webb or Snow I'll go ahead with my official complaint."

"You think Aidan will wait until then?"

"No. Where are you?"

Blazhevich decided there was no point in keeping the location a secret from his SIS contact. "Petropavlivska Borschagivka, I'm in the unfinished church."

Vickers knew the place, it had become somewhat of a landmark. Commissioned by a Kyiv businessman twelve years before and never completed, its large bell lay outside still wrapped in its protective cover. The bell proved too heavy and too sacred for anyone to run off with. "I'm here if you need me."

"Thanks." Blazhevich ended the call. There was movement at the front door. Through the magnified image of the stills camera he saw two Militia officers in shirt-sleeves smoking and grinning. One held a bottle of whisky and poured a shot for the other. Blazhevich muttered to himself as he took some more pictures. "Come on Aidan."

The cellar door opened and Kopylenko entered followed by another officer. The second officer spoke quietly into Kopylenko's ear. Kopylenko sneered and said. "Captain Budt would like to know how your head is Brian?"

"Tell him that his mother should be proud that he hits like a girl."

Snow sighed; Brian and Katya were both graduates of the same 'charm school'.

Kopylenko frowned. "I will tell him, it is serious. But a more serious matter is you, Mr Snow. You were not looking for Eric at all were you? No you came here because Brian called you. I have his phone and have also checked with immigration. So I have a question for you Mr Snow, who are you?"

"Why ask questions, just shoot him." Budt stated in Russian as he removed his side-arm from its holster and held it by his side.

Had he underestimated the men, would they try to kill him? Snow readied himself for action as he spoke. "I am Brian's friend. He asked me to come and here I am."

Kopylenko scratched his chin. "Now I believe what you are saying but that leaves us with a problem. You have assaulted a police officer. This is something that I cannot ignore so here is the deal. You will pay Captain Budt compensation of $15,000 and me another $15,000. We will take you to our personal banker. Once you have paid us I will personally drive you back to the airport."

"And what about Brian?"

"He must see the judge; his offence carries a much higher penalty."

"Why can't you just let it go man?" Webb stood, arms out at his sides and palms upwards trying to placate the policemen. "I am not the reason Katya left you. We both love Ana; we should be working this out together."

Kopylenko's face contorted with rage and he pointed angrily at Webb. "Because of you my daughter will not talk to me! I am her father! You have stolen her from me, from her grandparents and now you want to take her away for ever!"

"Think of her future, man."

"You have no future! Her future is here with me!" Kopylenko took a step forward. "Don't you understand? Now I can offer her the best. The Best! I have power, I have respect. I am no longer a simple officer from Donetsk."

"No you are a puppet."

Kopylenko struggled to control his anger and switched back to Russian. "Take them outside to the van. We shall move them to the woods and finish this."

Snow started to move but stopped when the Glock was aimed at his forehead. At point blank range he had no chance of avoiding a round. There was a tense silence which was broken by the Nokia ringtone.

Kopylenko pulled his phone from his pocket. "Da? Suka!" He swore. "Ruslan Fedorovich's is early. Move them quickly."

Budt nodded. "Ok."

Kopylenko left the room. Budt smiled, the Glock still trained at Snow's head. He now spoke in English, the accent all but incomprehensible. "Move now, up step. You one, you two. Now."

"Do what he says Brian."

Blazhevich had watched the owner return home in his dark green Bentley Continental GT. A long legged brunette had been in the passenger seat. The woman was not Imyets' wife. Blazhevich was getting more and more concerned for both Snow and his SBU investigation. He retrieved his mobile and started to dial Dudka's number when he saw a three car convoy approach the house. The lead and the last vehicle were matte black Mercedes G Wagons, most definitely AMG versions and most probably armour plated. The middle car was a piano-black Maybach 57S. There was something familiar about the convoy and Blazhevich frowned as he tried to remember who favoured that particular set up. The large gates opened once more and all three cars entered the courtyard. A bodyguard from each of the G-Wagons alighted, only then did a third suited man step out of the front of the Maybach and open the passenger door. A tall white haired figure dressed immaculately in a slate grey suit stepped out.

"Valeriy Ivanovich Varchenko" Blazhevich said to himself quietly as if not quite believing his own eyes. What was he doing here? Varchenko was a former KGB General and had been awarded the title 'Hero of the Soviet Union'. As Director Dudka's boss back in the days of the USSR he had remained one of the man's oldest friends. He was a member of the elite group nicknamed 'Nedotorkany' - 'the untouchables', oligarchs who played both sides of the law and as such were above it. They were friendly with Presidents and bandits alike. Blazhevich had met Varchenko, he didn't like him much. Whilst Blazhevich tried to make sense of what he saw the men moved into the house.

In the study Imyets had poured himself a large Cognac and was swirling it around in the bulbous glass as he listened to Kopylenko explain his presence. "Do you take me for a complete fool Pavel? Do you not think that I am aware of the petty racketeering that you and your men engage in under my protection?"

"No Ruslan Fedorovich."

"I make allowances for your little indiscretions, I even allowed you to go after this Englishman because I am a father, I have a heart and because in the past you have served me well. But now you bring him here, to my house? You bring your dirty laundry here to be cleaned?"

"I intended no offence, Ruslan Fedorovich. I am sorry."

Imyets downed the cognac then clicked his fingers. The brunette woman re-filled his glass. "Do you not see what you have done? You have signed their death warrant."

"But they have seen nothing…"

Imyets screamed. "Shut up! I cannot take that risk. I cannot let them leave this place. Do you not understand what I have here?"

Kopylenko had no idea what Imyets was talking about, to him it was just a house but his pride was such that he would not let on. "I am sorry…"

"Is that all you have to say? Pavel I trusted you, I offered you a real chance. Did I not bring you and your men to Kyiv with me?"

It was a rhetorical question but Kopylenko answered. "Yes you did."

Imyets drank some more then rolled his head from side to side. He had made a decision, he had no choice. "Pavel, you are sorry and I am truly sorry also. If only it had not ended like this."

Kopylenko was confused but realised that his life was in danger. "Ruslan Fedorovich please…"

"Bring in the Englishmen." Imyets ordered. The brunette nodded crossed to the door and several seconds later reappeared with Budt, Webb and Snow. Imyets switched to English and pointed at Webb. "You are the husband of his wife?"

"Er yes." Webb frowned.

"Who are you?" Imyets now pointed at Snow with his glass.

"His friend."

Imyets nodded. Placed his glass on his desk then opened a drawer. From this he produced an Uzi sub machine gun. "Say hello to my little friend!"

Snow's eye widened, Webb started to shake and the woman screamed. Imyets roared with laughter. "Do you really think that I would use this, in here, with all this hand crafted oak? No, even though it would make much less mess than an M203. So the question is what happens next?"

Snow held eye contact with the Politician. "Your men open the door and we go home."

Imyets shook his head. "No. It cannot happen. Pavel has made a mistake and I am sorry that all of you will pay."

Budt stepped forward and placed his Glock against Kopylenko's temple. Imyets picked up his glass and drank again. Snow and Webb stood motionless.

"No Officer Budt, do not do it here. You may ruin the rug. Just hit him."

Before Kopylenko could make any protest his former underling whacked him in the temple with the Glock and he instantly fell limp to the floor.
"Take him away. I shall call you with further instructions."
"Yes sir." Budt leant down and scooped Kopylenko up and over his shoulder.
"Now back to the Englishmen." Imyets sipped.
The doors to the study burst open to reveal Valeriy Varchenko. "You keep me waiting Imyets?"
Imyets smiled and raised his arms. "Business calls General. I am sorry but I have just been attending to a small problem."
Varchenko strode across the room then abruptly stopped when he saw Snow. "What is happening here?"
"These two men broke into my house. As you can see the Militia have made an arrest. I believe that they may have stolen some of my papers."
Varchenko fixed Imyets with an icy stare. "You will let these men go. They are under my protection."
"But General, they are under my roof."
"Yes and they are under my Krisha!"
Imyets looked confused. Even he dared not contradict Varchenko, a man who the President respected highly. "Then that is what I shall do Valeriy Ivanovich."
"Good." Varchenko turned to Snow. "Go home Aidan."
Snow nodded and grabbing Webb's arm hustled him out of the room.
Varchenko returned his gaze to Imyets. "Now are you going to insult me further by making an old man stand and not providing him with a drink?"
"Of course not, please." Imyets gestured to a large leather armchair.
"Thank you." Varchenko sat and the brunette brought him a glass of cognac. "Now a toast before we move onto more serious matters. Za nas, za vas, e za Donbas!"

'To us, to them and to Donbas'. Imyets approved of Varchenko's words.

Snow guided Webb into the hall and out of the front door. As he did so several large men in dark suits looked on impassively. Imyets own men however did not look pleased.
"Are you OK to walk?" Snow asked his friend as he helped him down the steps to the courtyard.
"I may be fat, bloodied and nursing a hangover but I am not a pensioner."
When they reached the gate it was opened for them. They stepped outside and it immediately shut. Snow breathed out a sign of relief. Webb slapped him on the back. "You did it Aidan, you got me out. But why did they let us go?"
"General Varchenko, I helped him once."
"You're a very helpful bloke aren't you Aidan?"
Snow chuckled. "Come on we've got to move. This way, towards the woods."
"You want to take me on a teddy bear's picnic?"
"Silly Sod."

Blazhevich waited around the corner by a path that led into the woods. Snow climbed into the front of the Passat and told Webb to get into the back.
As they moved off Blazhevich passed a can of beer to Webb. "You look like you need a drink."
"You must be my guardian angel." Webb pulled back the ring-pull and gulped down the Obolon.
After Snow had handled the introductions he said to Blazhevich, "I don't understand why Varchenko was there."
"Neither do I Aidan. I have no idea why, but you are lucky that he was." Blazhevich was also struggling to understand what all of this meant for his on-going investigation.
Snow thought back to the last time he had met Varchenko. It had been four years before and Snow had prevented a

paramilitary group from relieving Varchenko's bank of ten million dollars. Snow had been injured in the assault and Varchenko had visited him in hospital to give his thanks.
"Here, call your wife." Blazhevich handed Webb a mobile phone.
"Thanks, I'll just finish me can first or she'll smell the beer."
Snow looked at Blazhevich. "Did you see where they took Kopylenko?"
"Who?"
Snow explained as Webb spoke to Katya.
"I saw a Militia van leave a few minutes before you appeared. It was going deeper into the village."
Webb reached forward, handed the phone back to Blazhevich and then quickly grabbed Snow's head. He kissed him on the cheek. "That's from Katya."
"I won't ask if I get one." Blazhevich kept his eyes on the road as they headed back towards the city centre.
Snow wiped his cheek with his hand in mock disgust. "We need to go after Kopylenko. Imyets means to get rid of him."
Webb shrugged. "He is Ana's father after all, even though he is knob-head."
Blazhevich would have used a stronger term. "There is also the small issue of kidnapping but I agree, we need all the Intel we can get on Imyets. I'll get the boys back at HQ to ask officers Brovchenko and Klyuyev if they have any idea where Kopylenko may have been taken."
"Please do more than ask."
"Aidan, we are not going to water-board them."
"Pull over." Webb pointed. "There's an Apteka there and I feel like me skull's splitting open."
The Passat left the Zhytomyrska highway and glided into the bus station that served long distance travellers. All three men got out. The car was not parked in an official bay but its SBU number plate would avoid any fine or complaint.
"Can the SBU lend me some cash?"

"Here." Blazhevich handed Webb a two hundred Hryvnia note. He then shook his head and gave Snow one too. He retrieved his phone and stepped away to call HQ.

Webb gestured at a stall selling draft beer, snacks and water. "Get the drinks in lad, I'll be back in a mo."

Snow ordered two cans of 'Burn', a couple of 'Nuts Bars' and a half litre of Lvivski beer from the overly attractive girl and sat on the long green wooden bench seat that was affixed to the front of the concrete building. As he drank the energy drink and munched the chocolate he saw Blazhevich gesticulating into his phone and then to his right he heard raised voices. He glanced over. A thin drunk was waving his arms at a chubby woman who also appeared the worse for wear. She told him 'where to go' and stormed off, her tight jeans barely concealing her large buttocks. The drunk caught Snow's gaze and raised his plastic beer glass. Snow looked the other way but the man was not dissuaded and shuffled over.

"Where are you going?" The man asked in Ukrainian.

Snow looked up. "Nowhere."

The drunk laughed and tapped his chest. "Sergey."

"Sasha." Snow gave a false name; Aidan would mark him out as a foreigner.

Sergey swayed and then sat. "That woman you saw me with, she is a professional. You understand?"

"Yes."

"Sasha, did you like her? I could call her back. A real professional." He laughed and spilt some of his beer on his dirty jeans.

"He is a professional too." Snow pointed to Blazhevich who was walking towards them.

"Whatever you like you like." Sergey seemed puzzled and moved away.

"I think we'll have an address soon." Blazhevich stated as he sat.

"How soon?"

"Ten minutes perhaps. Where is Webb?"

Snow was suddenly worried but then relaxed as he saw the Yorkshire man nearing them carrying a plastic shopping bag.

Webb pointed at the beer. "Is that for me?"

Blazhevich looked him up and down. "You really need to get some medical attention."

Webb dropped down heavily next to them. "I'm gonna start now." He retrieved a bottle from the bag. "Dr Vodka."

"I'm serious Brian."

"So am I." Webb reached into his bag again and produced two packets of pills. He then proceeded to pop three ibuprofen and two paraceatamol tablets. These he washed down with the vodka straight from the bottle. "Ah that's better."

"How is the ankle?" Snow asked.

Webb held up his leg. "No ballet for a bit but I'll be ok. To be honest I think it's just a hangover. I'll soon drink it off."

The three men were silent for a moment as they watched a coach arrive and a stream of travellers walked in front on them. It was a stiflingly hot Sunday afternoon and Snow did not envy anyone travelling without air conditioning.

Blazhevich answered his phone. "Tak?" A smile spread across his face. "Dobre." He hung up. "The boys have worked their magic; apparently Brovchenko was very concerned that we may torture him."

"What a drip."

Blazhevich cast Snow a stern look. "So as I was about to say we have an address. There is a full tactical package in my boot, if you are interested?"

Snow stood. "Let's do it."

Stoyanka Village, Kyiv Oblast

The part of Stoyanka village where the target was being held was nicknamed 'Cuba' by the locals. Blazhevich did not know why. It was only three kilometres further along the Zhytomyrska highway than Imyets' house. It had originally consisted of a handful of Dachas on a large plane surrounded by a border of high trees. Over the past fifteen years however an ever growing number of three and four story houses had been built with new and dubious money. Half built houses and pegged out plots littered much of the remaining grassland. The address that officer Brovchenko had given up was one of the original Soviet era single story houses that had not yet been engulfed by new developments. It was on the edge of the village and faced the trees. A twenty-five minute drive from Kyiv's centre, with Militia lights flashing Kopylenko's men had used the house for 'nefarious' purposes. Blazhevich parked his Passat on the main road a quarter of a kilometre away from the target next to a second SBU vehicle. As ordered Webb stayed in the car and finished the remains of the chocolate and vodka. The SBU officer, who was already at the scene, shook hands with Blazhevich and then Snow before spreading a map across the bonnet of his Mazda.

"This is the target. As you can see it is on the edge of the village with one access road here. We can however gain access via the copse here."

Blazhevich asked his fellow operative. "How many men are inside Roman?"

"Victor and I have observed two men in the garden and other shadows inside. But we cannot confirm the number of hostiles."

"Victor has a visual now?"

Roman nodded. "He is in the trees directly opposite the dacha."

Blazhevich turned to Snow. "So Aidan, you have been better trained than us in hostage rescue techniques. What would the SAS do?"

HETMAN: DONETSK CALLING

"Go in, hard and fast and use the element of surprise. Roman, do you have schematics?"

"No. But it is a single story building."

Without Intel, planning and time, any assault would have an element of Heath Robinson about it. "OK. Here is my idea. We simultaneously throw flash-bangs in windows at the front and rear, but we go in through the rear. We clear each room and grab Kopylenko. They are Militia officers not terrorists, they do not expect to be attacked."

"Agreed but as they are not terrorists we are not shooting to kill. Roman, you and Victor will go to the front of the house and Aidan and I will take the rear. Fire warning shots, engage only if fired upon."

Snow smiled humourlessly. Not engaging an enemy was a recipe for disaster but Blazhevich was right, it would be senseless to kill members of the Militia, however corrupt they may or may not be.

"Suit up." Blazhevich commanded.

Blazhevich and Snow changed into digital camo overalls and all three men put on ballistic vests. Snow fastened a couple of stun grenades into his webbing and checked the Glock 22 he had retrieved from the tactical package.

Blazhevich took Snow to one side. "You do know that you are not actually officially here?"

"Yes and thank you." He respected the risk Blazhevich had taken in including him in the assault.

"Let's rock."

Snow supressed a laugh, Blazhevich had been watching too many Hollywood movies.

Silently they worked their way into the treeline as the late afternoon sun started to fade. Roman collected Victor and they skirted the target until they were concealed in the shadows opposite the front of the building caused by a half built house.

Blazhevich spoke to them via his throat mic once he and Snow were at the rear. "In position. Counting down. Three…Two…One…Go…Go…Go!"

As one Snow and Blazhevich hurled flash-bangs at the windows. Both men covered their ears and closed the eyes. The stun grenades shattered the glass and sailed inside before exploding with a deafening roar and a disorientating flash of white light. Milliseconds later Snow and Blazhevich climbed through the shattered glass, weapons up in a tactical stance. A woman, naked from the waist up screamed and moved away from a man who caught like a rabbit in head-lights sat frozen on a sofa, with an erection protruding like a weapon from his pants. Snow pistol-whipped him to the floor and moved further into the house. A doorway led to a narrow hallway and a two more doors. Blazhevich and Snow took a door each. Blazhevich's room was empty but Snow's contained the target. In the middle of the room Kopylenko sat, bound to a wooden chair.

"You?"

Captain Budt charged at Snow but the SIS operative was too fast. As Budt swung his fist Snow stepped outside the punch and simultaneously pushed down the arm with his own left forearm as he struck Budt's jaw with his hand still holding the Glock. Budt dropped, but Snow kicked him in the stomach for good measure. Snow searched the room in wide arcs and acquired a second target, another uniformed officer. The man instantly raised his arms. Snow took one step forward and kicked him in the groin then as he doubled up struck him on the back of the head with his Glock.

"Clear." Snow shouted as he stood and stared at Kopylenko.

"W...why?" The face of the Militia officer from Donetsk registered incomprehension.

Snow crouched in front of him. "You are Ana's father. Regardless of what I personally think about you I am not going to let a little girl I love, lose a parent."

"Th...thank you."
"Thank me and thank Brian."

Volodymyrska Street, Kyiv

Blazhevich shook Vickers' hand as the Diplomat let him into the flat. Both men moved to the lounge where Snow was sitting with a cup of coffee watching an infomercial for a vibrating foot massager.
"I see you are reacquainting yourself with Ukrainian television Aidan?
Snow smiled. "This is one of those channels that Alistair pays extra for."
"I do not." Vickers folded his arms.
Blazhevich smirked. "So I've come to give you an update."
Vickers grabbed the TV remote and switched the machine off. "Have a seat."
Blazhevich took an arm chair whilst Snow made room for his host. It was eleven a.m. Monday morning and Snow had spent the night at Vickers flat, giving Brian and Katya space to 'catch up'.
"Of the six men that we have in custody four have thus far provided us with intelligence regarding the 'activities' of Deputy Imyets."
"Do you have enough to bring formal charges?" Vickers asked.
"That is not an easy question to answer. We have the testimony of men who claim to take orders from Imyets but they are serving members of the Militia. I have agents looking into their claims and until we find anything concrete it is still their word against his."
"What about Kopylenko?" Snow asked.
"He acted under his own authority when he abducted Brian and held you."
"But Imyets ordered us done away with."

"True, but again it is his word and the word of those present against yours. In 'the west' perhaps things are easier and the rule of law prevails but I am afraid that in Ukraine 'Krisha' is everything. Imyets is protected by the President who in turn 'owns' the prosecutor's office. So unless we have a smoking gun and someone who will testify that they saw Imyets pull the trigger we are 'pissing into the wind'."

"And of course Vitaly if you share these same thoughts with the wrong people you may yourself be arrested for 'slandering the President'."

"You are right Alistair; our new laws get sillier and sillier every day."

"So what is to be done?" Snow now asked.

"The prisoners we have will be prosecuted on corruption charges unless they can come up with verifiable evidence against Imyets. The investigation will continue however I am sure Imyets will wash his hands of those men we have."

"What about Varchenko?"

Blazhevich let out a sigh. "Dudka has made it clear that the SBU is to not investigate or put any surveillance on Varchenko. This again makes me wonder what the General is doing with Imyets." Secretly Blazhevich also wondered if Dudka was holding back information from him but this was not something he wished to discuss with anyone.

"Vitaly, I'm sorry if I messed up your investigation."

"Aidan, you didn't mess it up. Shook it up perhaps, and perhaps we shall see if anything falls. So now that you have saved Webb what next?"

"Drinks."

Podil district, Kyiv

The small tented bar in Kyiv's Podil district was a favourite of Michael Jones. He let out a trail of smoke from his cigarette as he lazily stared at the cleavage of their waitress. "Great place, eh Aidan? Great place."

"Yep." Snow drank hungrily from his half litre beer glass. It was his first of the day and he had some catching up to do.

Jones' eyes followed the woman as she returned to the bar. "What more could you ask for? Great beer, great tits."

"Michael." Katya wagged her finger at the Welshman. "What would Ina say?"

"Oh, she would agree. She also likes tits."

Snow snorted into his beer. He had been away yet nothing had changed. His friends were still the same, and even though many bars had been renamed Kyiv was still Kyiv.

Webb raised his glass. "I would just like to say a toast to friendship, for without it we are all truly buggered!"

Katya nudged him in the belly. Snow and Michael both raised their glasses. "Buggered"

"Your friend Vitaly spoke to me today." Webb stated matter of fact. "He says that Kopylenko is now being very co-operative and wants to grant us permission to take Ana to the UK."

"That's good news."

"True but in return he wants me not to give evidence against him."

Snow raised his eyebrows. "So what are you going to do Brian?"

"He is going to give evidence and then when they put that idiot away a judge will of course let us take Ana to England." Katya crossed her arms.

Webb sipped his beer before winking at Snow. "That is what I am of course going to do."

Snow felt his Blackberry vibrate. It was a message from Patchem. He'd have to fly home in the morning but tonight he was home. Snow switched off his phone and ordered another round of drinks.

***

ALEX SHAW

Also by Alex Shaw in the Aidan Snow series:

HETMAN
A Special Forces Thriller introducing a reluctant hero, former SAS Trooper Aidan Snow.

Attacked by an unknown adversary, **Framed** for two assassinations, **Hunted** by the Ukrainian Security Service, the life of former SAS Trooper Aidan Snow has been destroyed.

Teaching at an international school in Ukraine, former SAS Trooper Aidan Snow has laid the nightmares of his past to rest. But when after ten years Snow meets again the man who put a gun to his head and ended his military career his past becomes very real.

Told by the British Secret Intelligence Service (SIS) that his would be tormenter is dead Snow tries to forget...

Attacked by an unknown adversary, Framed for two high profile assassinations and Hunted by the Ukrainian Security Service, Snow is torn from the life he has worked so hard to build and must once again rely on his SAS training in an attempt to clear his name.

Discovering a mercenary brigade made up of former Soviet Spetsnaz soldiers Snow trusts only himself to stop them and save those he cares about.
Snow is left one step ahead of the authorities with no one to watch his back.
In a Fire Fight, Pray for SNOW....

HETMAN: DONETSK CALLING

COLD BLACK – Hetman 2

Abduction
Veteran SAS trooper, Paddy Fox has lost his job, his wife and his temper. Whilst bitterly job hunting, Fox witnesses a car crash and finds himself rescuing a kidnapped Saudi Royal. Persuaded by MI6 to accept a job as security adviser in Saudi Arabia, Fox travels to Riyadh.

Assassination
In Kyiv, a director of the Belorussian KGB is gunned down whilst trying to pass shocking intelligence to his counterpart in the Ukrainian SBU. Intelligence, which if verified, sets out plans to commit international acts of terror.

Al-Qaeda
In Saudi Arabia, an entire British Trade mission is taken hostage by a new, highly funded, group aligned to Al-Qaeda. But who is funding this new insurgency and why?

An International Conspiracy
Former SAS Trooper turned MI6 operative, Aidan Snow is caught in a maelstrom involving East, West and Middle East which endangers the world's supply of oil.

Printed in Great Britain
by Amazon